The Chalk Doll

by Charlotte Pomerantz • Pictures by Frané Lessac

HarperCollins*Publishers*

The Chalk Doll
Text copyright © 1989 by Charlotte Pomerantz
Illustrations copyright © 1989 by Frané Lessac
Printed in China. All rights reserved.
Typography by Andrew Rhodes
For information address HarperCollins Children's
Books,a division of HarperCollins Publishers,
10 East 53rd Street, New York, NY 10022.

Library of Congress Cataloging-in-Publication Data
Pomerantz, Charlotte.
  The chalk doll.

  Summary: Rosy's mother remembers the pleasures of her childhood
in Jamaica and the very special dolls she used to play with.
  [1. Dolls—Fiction. 2. Mothers and daughters—Fiction.]
I. Lessac, Frané, ill. II. Title.
PZ7.P77Ch 1989   [E]   88-872
ISBN-10: 0-06-443333-1 (pbk.)
ISBN-13: 978-0-06-443333-4 (pbk.)

09 10 11 12 13 SCP 10

For Mary E. Woesner

Rose had a cold.
The doctor said to stay in bed
and try to nap during the day.
Rose's mother kissed her
and drew the curtains.
"You forgot to kiss me," said Rose.
"I did kiss you," said Mother.
"You didn't kiss me good night."
Mother went over and kissed her.
"Good night, Rosy," she said.
"I need my bear," said Rose.
"Your bear?" said Mother.

"You haven't slept with your bear
since you were little."
"I'm still little," said Rose.
She hugged her bear.
"Mommy," she said, "did you have
a bear when you were
a little girl in Jamaica?"
"No," said Mother. "But I had
a rag doll."

"I took a piece of material
and folded it over once.
With a pencil, I drew
the outline of the doll
on the material. Then I
cut along the outline and sewed
the two sides together.
Before I finished sewing
up the head, I stuffed the doll
with bits of rags."
"Did you like your rag doll, Mommy?"
"Yes, Rose, because I made it.
But I liked the dolls in
the shop windows more.
We called them chalk dolls."
"Did you ever have a chalk doll, Mommy?"

"Yes, my aunt worked for a family
who gave her a chalk doll,
and my aunt gave it to me.
The doll was missing an arm,
and her nose was broken."
"Poor doll," said Rose.
"Oh, no," said Mother.
"To me she was the most perfect
doll in the world."
"That's because she belonged to you,"
said Rose.
Mother smiled.
"Now try and rest," she said.
"I'll bring you a glass of milk."
Mother brought the milk.
Rose drank half, then looked up.
"Did you like milk when you
were a little girl?"

"I loved milk," said Mother.
"But the milk was different.
It came in a can and it was
sweeter and thicker.
Every morning, my mother
took out two tablespoons
and dropped them into the tea.
We all got a taste. After breakfast,
Mother would cover the can with foil
and hide it."
"Where did she hide it, Mommy?"
Mother shrugged.
"I never found out," she said. "But
I watched her every morning. And
I dreamed that one day, when I grew up,
I was going to buy a whole can
and drink it all."
"Did you?" said Rose.

Mother was quiet.
"No," she said finally.
"I never thought about it
till just now."
"Tell me another story," said Rose.
"I can't think of any," said Mother.
"Tell me the story of your
birthday party."
Mother looked puzzled.
"My birthday party?
We didn't have birthday parties."
"What about the three pennies?"
said Rose.
"Oh," said Mother. "That time."

"On the day I was seven years old,
my mother gave me three pennies.
I had never had so much money.
The pennies were cool
and smooth in my hand.
I went to a store and bought a
little round piece of sponge cake
for a penny. Then I went to
another store and bought a
penny's worth of powdered sugar.
In the third store, I bought six
tiny candies for a penny.

When I got home, I sprinkled
powdered sugar on the top."
"I bet I know what happened then,"
said Rose. "Five friends came
over. You cut the cake into
six little pieces
and you had a party.... But Mommy,
you didn't get any presents."
"No, I never did."
"Never, never?"
"Well," said Mother, "I did,
if you count the pink taffeta dress."

"My mother was a seamstress.
She worked at home, sewing
for other people.
One year she brought home some
pink taffeta. Pink taffeta
was my favorite.
She said she would try
and make me a dress
for my birthday.
But she was so busy
sewing dresses for other people
that weeks and weeks went by
and she still hadn't touched
the pink taffeta.
The night before my birthday,
I went to bed hoping she would
make the dress while I was asleep.
But when I woke up,
the pink taffeta material
was still there.
I went to the yard and cried."

Rose leaned over
and hugged her mother.
"Poor Mommy," she said.
"Did she ever make the dress?"
"Yes," said Mother.
"She finished the dress
a month after my birthday.
It was the most beautiful dress I ever had."
"What kind of shoes did you
wear with it, Mommy?"
"No shoes, Rose.
We only wore shoes
to church on Sunday."
"You mean you went to school barefoot?"
"Yes," said Mother. "Nobody
wore shoes except the teacher...
But I *did* wear high heels."

"The road to and from school
was paved with tar, and
there were mango trees
on both sides.
We ate the sweet fruit
and dropped the pits.
They dried in the sun.
We took the dried pits
and rubbed them into
the tar on the road.
The tar was soft and sticky.

After we rubbed the mango pits
in the tar, we pressed
the sticky pits
against the heels of our feet
until they stuck.
Then we walked home
clickety click clacking
on our mango heels."
Rose smiled.
"Clickety click clack," she said.
"You had fun when you were
a little girl, didn't you, Mommy?"

"Yes, Rosy. I did."
"Do I have as much fun
as you did?" Rose asked.
"Mm," said Mother,
"what do you think?"
"I think I have fun too,"
said Rose. "But there is one thing
I'd like to have that you had."
Rose got out of bed
and went to the sewing basket
in the hallway.
She took out a needle and thread,
a pair of scissors, and some
scraps of material.
"What are you doing?" said Mother.
"I'm getting everything ready."
"Ready for what, Rose?"

"Ready to make a rag doll."
"But Rose," said Mother,
"you have so many dolls."
"I know," said Rose.
"But they are all chalk dolls.
I've never had a rag doll."
Mother laughed.
"Poor Rosy," she said.
And together they made
a rag doll.